J May
May, Kyla
Mika : my new life

$15.99
ocn834433191
10/30/2013

Mika

My New Life

READ ALL THE LOTUS LANE BOOKS!

LOTUS LANE

Mika

My New Life

by Kyla May

BRANCHES

SCHOLASTIC INC.

To my mum, who encouraged me to be imaginative.
To my dad, who taught me to work hard.
To my husband, who makes me laugh and love.

Library of Congress Cataloging-in-Publication Data
May, Kyla, author, illustrator.
Mika : my new life / written and illustrated by Kyla May.
pages cm — (Lotus Lane ; 4)
Summary: Japanese American Mika is the newest member of the Lotus Lane Girls, with
her very own new diary, but she is still troubled by tensions between her different friends,
and worried about her project for the school newspaper.
ISBN 978-0-545-49620-9 (hardcover) — ISBN 978-0-545-44519-1 (pbk.) 1. Japanese American
families—Juvenile fiction. 2. Student newspapers and periodicals—Juvenile fiction. 3. Diaries—Juvenile
fiction. 4. Best friends—Juvenile fiction. 5. Friendship—Juvenile fiction. 6. Elementary schools—Juvenile
fiction. 7. Diary fiction. [1. Japanese Americans—Fiction. 2. Family life—Fiction. 3. Newspapers—Fiction. 4.
Diaries—Fiction. 5. Best friends—Fiction. 6. Friendship—Fiction. 7. Elementary schools—Fiction. 8. Schools—
Fiction.] I. Title.
PZ7.M4535Mik 2013
813.6—dc23
2013011628

ISBN 978-0-545-49620-9 (hardcover) / ISBN 978-0-545-44519-1 (paperback)

12 11 10 9 8 7 6 5 4 3 2 1   13 14 15 16 17 18/0

Printed in China
First Scholastic printing, November 2013

38

TABLE OF CONTENTS

THIS
DIARY
BELONGS TO

MiKA

Chapter 1

**Surprise!
Surprise!**

Thursday

Dear Diary,

This is so exciting! I have my
very own diary! And it was given
to me by my new friends Kiki,
Coco, and Lulu.

You don't know this about me
yet, Diary, but I just came to
the United States from Japan.
I wasn't expecting to make friends quickly
because I am <u>SO</u> shy, but I guess I did. Yay!

Speaking of which . . . I'd better text my new friends right now to thank them for this surprise gift!

Mika_msg

Mika: Thank you so, so, so much! You shouldn't have! (But I'm glad you did!)

I still can hardly believe you're here, Diary! I was so not expecting you. My family all went out to dinner earlier tonight to celebrate the

Dad's restaurant

opening of my dad's new restaurant. His name is Sei Maeda, and the restaurant is called Sei Sushi. Anyway, when we got home, there was a pretty gift bag with my name on it by the front door!

my front door

gift bag

And when I looked inside that bag, there you were – with a card signed by Kiki, Coco, and Lulu. They each have a diary, so it feels extra special that they thought to give me one, too.

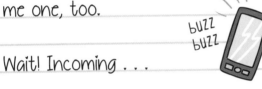

TO Mika
Love,
Kiki,
Coco,
and Lulu

Wait! Incoming . . .

buzz buzz

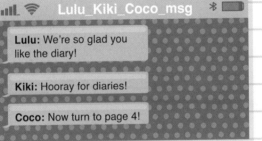

Lulu_Kiki_Coco_msg

Lulu: We're so glad you like the diary!

Kiki: Hooray for diaries!

Coco: Now turn to page 4!

Hmmm . . . I wonder what's on page four?

YOU ARE INVITED TO
THE LLGC PAJAMA PARTY!

WHEN: TOMORROW NIGHT

WHERE: COCO'S HOUSE

BRING: A SLEEPING BAG,
A TOOTHBRUSH,
AND PAJAMAS

This is so exciting! I can't wait! Wait — I just realized you don't know what the LLGC is. Sorry, Diary!

LLGC stands for Lotus Lane Girls Club. It's made up of:

Lulu, who loves Penelope Glitter from the Sleuth Sally movies and has a cat named Bosco;

Lulu & Bosco

Kiki, who loves fashion and has a dog named Maxi;

Kiki & Maxi

and Coco, who loves baking and has a dog named Evie and a cat named Lucky.

Coco, Lucky, and Evie

These girls are all best friends, and they live on Lotus Lane, where I live, too. Their club has a different activity almost every day, and on Friday nights, they always have a Pajama Party.

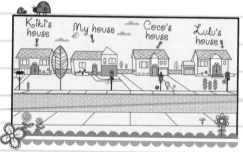

Kiki's house   My house   Coco's house   Lulu's house

I'm so excited I might not be able to fall asleep! As we say in Japan, **oyasumi-nasai.** (oh -ya-su-mi na-sai)

OYASUMI-NASAI = "good night" in Japanese

Chapter 2

New News

Friday

Good morning!

Diary, in all my excitement yesterday, I forgot to tell you about my family.

I hope you don't think I'm <u>this</u> rude all the time. It's more like when Penelope Glitter won Best Actress at the Teen Movie Awards and forgot to thank her parents in her speech. Of course she meant to, but in all the excitement, it just slipped her mind!

So my dad is really tall and his head is completely bald. The food he makes is delicious! And he always wears green plastic clogs. Always!

See?

My mom is an interior decorator. She decorates inside people's homes. This is what she looks like.

And my grandma lives with us. She is very old, and very, very smart. She sees everything. As my mother says, "she has eyes in the back of her head."

Okay . . . Let's see. . . . What else can I tell you about myself?

LIKES:

hip-hop rocks

- ♥ Hip-hop dancing
  (My favorite thing in the whole wide world.)

 YUM

- ♥ Sushi

BOB

- ♥ Bob (I ♥ my dog!)

- ♥ Drawing

- ♥ Sleuth Sally movies

- ♥ My Zen garden

ZEN =
of a quiet
mind, peaceful

A Zen garden is a garden made of sand, small rocks, plants, and trees. You rake the sand into wave shapes so it looks like the sea or a river. I go sit in my Zen garden when I need to think or when I feel a little homesick for Japan.

Oh - I better run or I'll be late for school!

I'm back! Miss me?

So, Diary, there's one other person I have to tell you about. . . . Her name is Katy Krupski. She was the first person at school to talk to me . . .

I like your sunglasses.

Thank you.

. . . and the first person to invite me to hang out after school.

Everything seemed great . . . until a couple of weeks ago when I left my phone at her house. I later found out Katy had read my texts. SO not nice.

Katy has said mean things to Kiki, Coco, and Lulu, so they don't like her. They call her the Queen of Mean (not to her face, though!). I'm not sure if I still want to be Katy's friend or not - now that I'm friends with the Lotus Lane Girls (the LLGs).

Katy

LLGs

At school today, our teacher gave us a big project due Monday. We each have to turn in something for the school newspaper. Kiki's doing a fashion report, Coco's creating a recipe, and Lulu's writing a movie review.

My teacher, Miss Humphries

I want to draw a comic - if I can do a good enough job. As I said earlier, I love drawing! **Kawaii** (kuh-why-ee) is a very cute and comic-like style of drawing that I love.

KAWAII = "cute" in Japanese

Some people say that the trick to drawing kawaii-style faces is to put the eyes very close to the mouths. You can make almost anything kawaii style just by putting a face on it - even something not cute at all, like a toaster or a book. See?

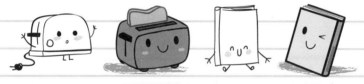

I have to work really hard on this comic. Miss Humphries said that the first part of this project doesn't have to be final. We just have to show her what we're hoping to do for the newspaper. Then she'll tell us if we can do it FOR REAL or not. EEK!

During lunch today, Kiki, Coco, and Lulu were all wondering what Katy might submit for the newspaper:

"A question and answer for phone spies?"
— Kiki

"An advice column for bullies?" — Lulu

"A top-ten list of mean things to say?"
— Coco

"Um . . ." — me

I hope the LLGs don't mind that I'm still Katy's friend.

Okay, I'd better get ready for tonight's Pajama Party. The girls said they have a big surprise for me! I'll tell you all about it tomorrow!

Chapter 3

Lotus Lane Love

LOTUS LANE

Saturday

Last night was so much fun! And <u>SO</u> surprising. Take a good look, Diary, at the newest member of the LLGC! That's right, last night I became the fourth Lotus Lane Girl!!!!!!!!!!!!!!!!!!!!!!!!!!!!

So last night, I walked into Coco's bedroom and saw this banner:

WELCOME TO
THE LOTUS LANE GIRLS CLUB, MIKA!
WE'RE SO HAPPY TO HAVE YOU!

"But <u>you're</u> the LLGs." – me

"That's right." – Kiki

"You want <u>me</u> to be a Lotus Lane Girl, too?" – me

"Yes." – Coco

"That's kind of why we made the banner." – Kiki

I was so nervous - and excited! Then I said the LLGC oath:

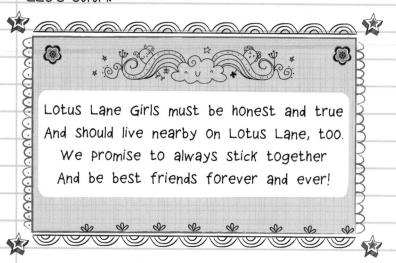

Lotus Lane Girls must be honest and true
And should live nearby on Lotus Lane, too.
We promise to always stick together
And be best friends forever and ever!

Then we all started jumping up and down so hard that Coco's uncle Nick yelled at us to stop. Then I was a <u>real</u> member of the LLGC.

Oh . . . look at the time, Diary. It's almost eleven a.m. or on LLGC time, Cupcake Catch-Up O'Clock! Cupcake Catch-Up is another LLGC weekly activity! **TTYL!**

TTYL = talk to you later

Cupcake Catch-Up was so great! We decorated cupcakes and I showed my friends how to draw kawaii-style characters on top of cupcakes. Want to see a picture?

We also talked about our newspaper projects. As I was leaving, the girls reminded me that the LLGC has their Super Scrapbooking activity after school on Monday. I can't wait!!

Diary, have you ever heard of Harajuku fashion? It started in the Harajuku area of Tokyo, which is a fashion capital of the world. Harajuku Girls dress up in funky outfits.

I was just reading my brand-new magazine, *Harajuku Girl*, which is full of awesome new outfits.

These styles would look good on the LLGs, too.

I could see Kiki in a pink wig! And maybe she'd wear this pink baby-doll dress.

Lulu might like this black lipstick! And this long black dress and platform boots would look amazing on her!

and Coco might like this blond wig, and this cute pair of cutoff shorts.

I would dress up as a rock star with this black leather jacket and super-skinny plaid pants.

I predict Harajuku dreams. . . .

Chapter 4

Paw Prints

Sunday

Good morning, Diary!

For breakfast, my dad made tomato spinach omelets and green smoothies for brain power . . . which I really need right now! I STILL haven't come up with an idea for my comic, which is due tomorrow!!!

Mom is busy painting the white fence around her flower garden. And my grandmother is busy sewing. So now is the perfect time to think about my comic!

Hold on . . . my phone is ringing.

Well, Diary, Katy called earlier and asked if she could come over. I thought maybe she could help me think of an idea for my comic, so I said sure. Now I'm covered in white paint and feeling yucky. UGH! Let me explain. . . .

Katy was not at all helpful. She showed me her project for the school newspaper, and IT WAS A GOSSIP COLUMN! She had written all kinds of things in there!

I think most of the stuff she wrote was meant to be funny, not really mean. But, Diary, there was this <u>one</u> thing she wrote. . . .

Remember how I told you that Lulu loves the actress who plays Sleuth Sally? Well, a couple weeks ago, both Lulu and Katy entered and won a Sleuth Sally Look-Alike Contest. (Go, Lulu and Katy!)

Part of their prize was that they got tickets to the new Sleuth Sally movie, **Double Trouble**, and they could bring friends. So, Kiki and Coco went with Lulu, and I went with Katy. (And a girl named Jada came, too, but that's another story.) Anyway, we all took a picture together on the red carpet. And, well, Coco does not care about fashion AT ALL.

So, on the red carpet, let's just say Coco was a total "fashion-do" from the ankles up. . . .

But from the ankles down, a major "fashion-don't". . . . She was wearing socks with sandals.

And in the gossip column, this is what Katy wrote under the red-carpet photo:

Coco Corvino:
Dressed for the red carpet or for her grandparents' picnic?

It made me so angry, my
ears were burning!

"Why would you show that
to me? Coco is my friend!" I shout-asked her.
I've never raised my voice to Katy before. I'm
not even sure I've _ever_ raised my voice.

Katy didn't say anything. She just left. I'm
starting to think that Kiki, Coco, and Lulu are
right about her . . . She's the Queen of Mean.

I was thinking about what happened, when
all of a sudden, Bob burst into my room! He
jumped up all over me and covered me in white
paw prints. He must have stepped in my mom's
white paint! Doesn't that big ol' clumsy mutt
know that I have more important things to
do than clean up after him? Like come up with
a comic stri-

WAIT A MINUTE . . . Bob just gave me an idea
for my comic!

Ta-Daa!

Like it?

I hope Miss Humphries likes this comic enough
to let me draw a REAL comic for the school
newspaper. I guess I'll find out soon enough....
Sleep tight.

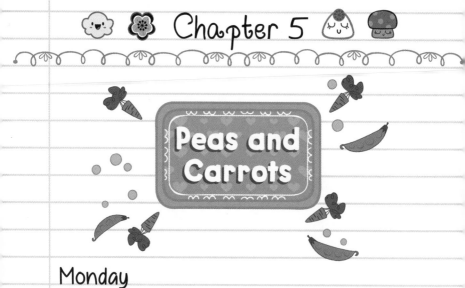

Chapter 5

Peas and Carrots

Monday

Hi, Diary! Sorry I couldn't say hello this morning, but I was busy finishing my comic of Bob before school. I'm still worried that it won't be good enough.

The only person who saw it was Katy. She looked over my shoulder as I stood in line to hand it in.

"Cute." – Katy

Cute? One word? She didn't even say it like she meant it!

Are you thinking what I'm thinking, Diary?

Keep in mind, it's Katy. She's the Queen of Mean.

That might be true. But how can I be sure?

After that happened, I wandered down to lunch in a foggy cloud. And I walked straight into someone's food tray! Peas and carrots went flying everywhere.

"I'm sorry. Oh no — here, let me get that . . .
Jada? Oh! Jada! It's you!" – me

(Long pause as I stare at her, mouth wide
open. A pea lands on my tongue.)

"mika?!" – Jada

Jada

The reason I was so surprised to see Jada,
Diary, is because she goes to my hip-hop class,
but she's never gone to this school before.

Lulu met Jada first. She actually helped Jada
adopt a dog named Ada. Then Jada came to
the Sleuth Sally movie with all of us, and she
also joined my hip-hop class.

Jada and I must
have been **shricking**
loudly because the LLGs
rushed right over to us.

SHRIEKING =
yelling loudly

LOTUS LANE

And guess what, Diary!
Jada has moved to our
town. And now she lives
on Lotus Lane! Is that
crazy or what?!

We all ate lunch together. I was having so
much fun until I noticed Katy looking over
from the next table. Even though she was
sitting with her friends, she didn't look happy.
That made me feel kind of crummy.

Then, when we all got up to leave, Jada said, "Bye, Mika! See you tonight at hip-hop!"

"HipHopTonight?WhatAboutSuperScrapbooking?"
— Kiki, Coco, and Lulu

*Hip-hop class?! How could
I have forgotten?!*

Super Scrapbooking is the
LLGC Monday night activity. But
Monday night is also when I have hip-hop class.
And, as you know, hip-hop is my most favorite
activity EVER!

The LLGs said I should go to hip-hop today.
But what if they didn't mean it? And what if
they somehow find out about what Katy wrote
about Coco in her gossip column? They might
get really upset with me since they think I'm
Katy's friend (which may or may not be true).

So now I'm going to hip-hop class. Hope for
the best, Diary.

Chapter 6

Fashion Police

Tuesday

Rise and shine, Diary!

Hip-hop class was so much fun last night! We practiced our new **routine** and I didn't make one mistake. Not one!

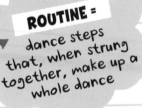

ROUTINE = dance steps that, when strung together, make up a whole dance

Our teacher even moved me up to the front row so the girls who weren't so sure of the steps could follow me. Jada was already up front, so it was cool that both of us got to be there together.

I hope the LLGs didn't have too much fun at Super Scrapbooking without me . . . and that they weren't talking about what a big mistake they made inviting me into their club.

Today at school, I'm going to find out whether my Bob comic was good enough for Miss Humphries to let me do a real comic for the school newspaper. Keep your fingers, er, pages, crossed, Diary!

Diary, the most stressful thing just happened! I was standing with the LLGs when Katy walked up to me.

"You can relax, Mika. Miss Humphries said no to my gossip column. I'm doing an events calendar instead." — Katy

Katy walked away. But Kiki, Coco, and Lulu were all looking at me.

"Katy wrote a gossip column?" – **Kiki**

"Did Katy write something about you? Or about one of us?" – **Lulu**

"Mika, do you know something we don't know?" – **Coco**

Being the shy person I am, I'm nervous just talking to people. But talking to people and saying things that aren't true? That's pretty much impossible. So I told them EVERYTHING.

Kiki and Lulu were upset. But, surprisingly, Coco didn't care. In fact, she calmed the other two down. Katy said something mean about Coco's baking once - Coco was furious then because baking is super important to her. But she doesn't care about fashion, so she's not embarrassed to be called out on her poor fashion sense.

I was so relieved. If Coco's feelings had been hurt, she might have been mad at me since I didn't tell her about the gossip column to begin with. But since she didn't really care, she dropped it. And Kiki and Lulu understood why I hadn't said anything earlier.

The really important thing is that Miss Humphries shut Katy down - like I'd hoped she would. So Katy's gossip column won't be in the newspaper.

I was still upset about what Katy had written in her column, though. So I took all my shyness - of which I have a LOT - and pretended it was actually **courage**. Then I went to find Katy. . . .

COURAGE = bravery

"Katy, if you can't be nice to my new friends, then I just can't be friends with you anymore." – me

Then I melted into a
puddle of fear.

And Katy stormed off down the hall.

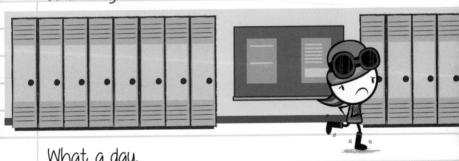

What a day.

Wait! I forgot to tell you the most important
thing: Miss Humphries said I can do the comic
for the school newspaper. All the LLGs can do
their projects, too. HOORAY!!!!!

I'm off to Doggie
Day Spa now. . . .

HOORAY!!!

HOORAY!!!

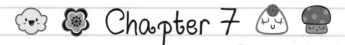

Chapter 7

There Are No Bad Ideas
(. . . unless you're me)

Wednesday

Hello, Diary! Doggie Day Spa was awesome yesterday! We gave all of our pets bubble baths and talked about our newspaper projects.

And, while brushing Bob, I offered to host this Friday's Pajama Party. I'm so excited! Now I just have to think of a **theme** for it. (One time, the LLGs had a Sleuth Sally-themed sleepover where they watched Sleuth Sally movies and dressed up like her character!)

THEME = a subject or topic

Maybe an idea for the greatest theme EVER will come to me on the walk to school. . . .

Sleuth Sally-themed costume

The only thing I thought of on my walk to school was all my worries. On top of a Pajama Party theme, I have to come up with an idea for my real comic. Miss Humphries said my Bob comic was great, but I want to create something EVEN GREATER for the newspaper!

At lunch today, I told the LLGs I was having trouble coming up with an idea for my comic. Lulu suggested I write a list of all of my ideas and then pick the best one. Lulu loves lists.

So, during recess, I took out a piece of paper and wrote:

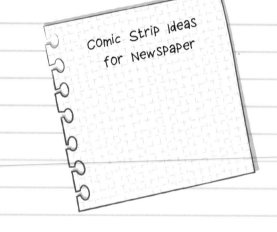

Comic Strip Ideas for Newspaper

I stared at the blank page for a while.

"Don't worry, Mika, you'll come up with something good. You're so creative," said a voice that sounded like Katy Krupski's.

When I looked up, Katy was standing right in front of me. I thanked her for what she'd just said. Then she said, "You're welcome," and quietly walked away.

I kind of wish I hadn't said what I said about our friendship yesterday. But I'm feeling like it may be too late to do anything about that now.

I couldn't concentrate on my list after that.

Diary, remember when you were only a baby diary and things were going so well for us? **WELL, THOSE DAYS ARE OVER!!!**

Today's LLGC activity was Ten-Minute Makeover. I started practicing Harajuku styles of makeup on everyone.

As I was working on Kiki's baby-doll look, Coco took pictures of us.

"We should print these photos and use them for next monday's Super Scrapbooking meeting." – **Kiki**

"Awesome idea, Kiki!" – **Lulu**

"That's cuckoo bananas!" – **Coco**

"Great. But I might be in hip-hop class."
— Little Voice Inside My Head

I got really quiet. The girls could tell I was upset about something, and Lulu figured it out right away.

"Oh no ... Mika, you're not going to be at Super Scrapbooking, are you?" — Lulu

"I didn't say that. . . ." — me

"You mean you _are_ going to be there?"
— Coco

"I didn't say _that_ either." — me

"Maybe we should talk about something else? Have you come up with the Pajama Party theme?" — Kiki

That's when things went from bad to worse. I told them my possible themes and they hated all my ideas. Here are a couple of them:

Super Listing—
We could write lists and lists and more lists!

Salad Catch-Up—
This would be like Cupcake Catch-Up, but healthier!

"um..." – Kiki

"I second that." – Coco

"Potato chip?" – Lulu

I get it. These ideas aren't great. Also, they totally stink.

I got really quiet after that. I couldn't even finish Kiki's makeover.

Oh boy. My head is swirling. . . . Ideas for the Pajama Party theme, ideas for my comic, and ideas for how on earth I can possibly be at hip-hop class and Super Scrapbooking at the same time on Monday.

I wonder if I'll be able to fall aslee-

Chapter 8

You Feel Bad . . . I Feel Sad

Thursday

I am so sorry! How impolite of me to fall asleep on you, Diary! I didn't realize how tiring it can be to come up with terrible ideas. Please accept my apology.

Thank you! I'll talk to you after school. . . .

Oh, Diary! I had kind of a sad talk with Katy during recess today. Soon I'm going to have to start calling recess "Katy and Mika time."

Anyway, I was sketching in my notebook, still trying to figure out what to do for my comic. All I had were pictures of flowers with faces on them, like these:

Well, Katy passed me and said, "Those drawings are really cute, Mika."

I thanked her. Then, before I could think of anything to say, she apologized to me for writing about Coco in her gossip column! She said she only did it because she was jealous that I was spending more and more time with the LLGs and less and less time with her.

"I thought if you saw what bad style Coco has, you might see that those girls aren't as cool as I am. And then you'd want to hang out with me instead." — **Katy**

"But there's more to friendship than clothes or being cool." — me

"I know it was sort of silly to think that."
— **Katy**

I thanked Katy for her honesty. But I told her I would still have to think about whether I can be friends with her anymore. She looked sad, which made me feel bad.

I'm going to go sit in my Zen garden now. I really need to think about things.

I sat and thought.

It wasn't helpful.

I tried raking the sand into waves, but they kept coming out like question marks.

Then I drew all the things that are worrying me right now: Katy, my comic, hip-hop, and scrapbooks.

Bob found me and started scratching at my hip-hop drawing. I guess we know his vote. I just don't know what to do. Plus, I still haven't picked a theme for the Pajama Party, which is tomorrow night!!!

Diary, how about you be me and I be you?

No? You're right. . . .
I guess that won't work.

Chapter 9

When It Rains, It Pours

Friday

Oh, Diary, I'm so tired! I was **tossing and turning** all night.

> **TOSSING AND TURNING =**
> when you can't sleep at night

Anyway, Dad's calling me for breakfast. . . .

This day did not get off to a good start. Here's what happened at breakfast. . . .

"I made your favorite sushi
for you for lunch today."
— Dad, pointing to my lunch box

"UGH! I don't want sushi again!!!"
— me, yelling at Dad

"CRRREEEAAK."
— My poor dad's heart, breaking

"I wish I hadn't said that."
— Little Voice Inside My Head,
one second later

I feel terrible for yelling at Dad. I love sushi. And I love Dad. I just yelled at the wrong person. But you can't exactly yell at yourself, can you . . . ? Not even when you're messing up big-time. Well, I have to leave for school . . . deep breaths . . .

Recess was no fun today. The LLGs were all so excited about their newspaper projects. And then there was me. . . .

Right before class started again, Katy waved at me and I waved back. The girls all saw this, so I felt like I should tell them about Katy's apology from yesterday.

"I guess if any of you suddenly started hanging out with someone new, I might try to stop you from liking them, too."
— Coco

55

"Knowing that she was feeling jealous does kind of change things." – Kiki

"Mika, you'll just have to decide if you can trust her as a friend again." – Lulu

The girls shared their sandwiches with me at lunch. (After my sushi **tantrum**, I forgot mine!)

TANTRUM = a fit, yelling and screaming

"Where's your usual delicious sushi?" – Kiki

I told them about yelling at my dad – and about how I was actually mad at myself, not my dad.

"Why?" – Coco

"For not being able to come up with ideas for tonight's Pajama Party theme or for my comic strip, and for not being able to be at hip-hop class and Super Scrapbooking at the same time." – me

They told me I was trying too hard to come up with a Pajama Party theme that I thought they would want to do. They told me to think of something I would like to do instead.

"That's why we all get along so well. Because we do things we love and we try things the other girls love, too." – Lulu

I felt so much better, but I still had to think of a theme and I still didn't know what to do about my comic strip, or about Super Scrapbooking and hip-hop class.

Then this happened:

"Wait a second! I just thought of the answer! That thing I just said about trying things the other girls love?" – Lulu

"That's what we should do with your hip-hop class, Mika!"
— Coco, finishing Lulu's thought

"Yes! We can move Super Scrapbooking to Thursdays instead! That way we can all try hip-hop!" – Lulu

And then suddenly I had an idea for tonight's Pajama Party. Something I really love to do, but I haven't even thought about since leaving Japan.

Until now . . .

Something <u>so</u> good, I'm going to keep it a surprise. Even from you, Diary.

Shhhhhhhh...

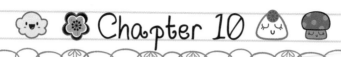

Chapter 10

Did Someone Say Karaoke?

Saturday

Okay, Diary! The moment we've all been waiting for . . . The theme for last night's Pajama Party was . . . KARAOKE! (This is a funny-looking word, and it's pronounced "carry-oh-key.")

That's right . . .
you heard me . . .
KARAOKE!

I've been so busy that I forgot all about one of my favorite things in the whole wide world: my **karaoke machine**!

I even have a karaoke CD for songs from the Sleuth Sally movies. It includes ten songs from *Sleuth Sally the Musical*!

KARAOKE MACHINE = a screen that displays song lyrics, plus a microphone for singing along

So last night we dressed up like Sleuth Sally and sang until my grandma told us we were keeping her awake. Then we watched *Sleuth Sally the Musical* and ate popcorn until our stomachs almost exploded.

Kiki, Coco, and Lulu LOVED my theme! Oh, and they loved the new LLGC activity schedule I made, too! It has hip-hop class on Monday nights and Super Scrapbooking on Thursdays. Hooray!!! Check it out!

	MONDAY	TUESDAY	WEDNESDAY
Club Name	Hip-Hop Class	Doggie Day Spa	Ten-Minute Makeover
Club Activity	Learn hip-hop dance routines	Pamper our pets	Do manicures, pedicures, and style our hair
Club Location	Amber Acres Dance School	Coco's backyard	Lulu's bedroom

LOTUS LANE GIRLS CLUB SCHEDULE

THURSDAY	FRIDAY	SATURDAY	SUNDAY
Super Scrapbooking	Pajama Party	Cupcake Catch-Up	LOTUS DAY OFF
Create scrapbook pages	Watch movies, eat popcorn, gossip	Bake cupcakes	
Kiki's house	Kiki's, Lulu's, Coco's or Mika's house	Coco's kitchen	

I'm really lucky my parents moved us to this house on Lotus Lane or I might never have gotten to know Kiki, Coco, and Lulu.

Now it's time for Cupcake Catch-Up.

Cupcake Catch-Up was amazing! We each made a cupcake to match the country our family comes from.

I made cupcakes with **mochi** on top.

MOCHI = a Japanese bubble-like topping made from rice

my cupcake

Coco drew green, white, and red stripes on top of her cupcake. It looked like a little Italian flag!

coco's cupcake

Lulu drew a mini Eiffel
Tower (a really cool building
in Paris, France!) on hers.

Lulu's cupcake

And Kiki made a cute little
lotus flower on her cupcake — for
Lotus Lane! (Yes, Diary, we know
Lotus Lane isn't a <u>real</u> country. . . .)

Kiki's cupcake

It's been such a great day! BUT I'm
still feeling awful about yelling at Dad yesterday
and just haven't gotten to talk to him about
it yet. I <u>REALLY</u> have to apologize!!!!

Well, Diary, I finally apologized. Here's what Dad
said after I said I was sorry:

> **"Change is good for the soul, but sometimes
> it takes time to embrace change."**

This means he knows how hard the move from Japan has been for me, and he thinks it's just taking me some time to get comfortable here. He said he thinks I'm doing a pretty great job, though. And I promised to talk with him next time about what's <u>really</u> worrying me instead of yelling at him about sushi.

I feel so much better knowing that Dad isn't upset with me!

NOW IF I COULD JUST FIGURE OUT WHAT TO DO FOR MY COMIC, EVERYTHING WOULD BE PERFECT!

Chapter 11

Five-Girl Pileup

Sunday

Good morning, Diary. Did you happen to think of what to do for my comic strip?

Me neither . . .

Hold on! My phone is ringing. *RING!*

Jada just called. She wants to come over to practice our hip-hop routine for class tomorrow. I said sure. Maybe dancing will shake the idea loose from my brain.

Wait . . . now my phone is buzzing.

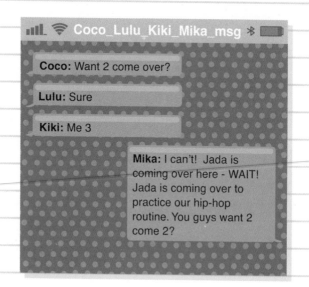

Coco: Want 2 come over?

Lulu: Sure

Kiki: Me 3

Mika: I can't! Jada is coming over here - WAIT! Jada is coming over to practice our hip-hop routine. You guys want 2 come 2?

Everyone was at my house in a flash!

Jada and I tried to teach the LLGs our routine from class. They were really good. Well, except when Kiki had to look at her hand to remind herself which direction is left and which is right. She makes an L shape with her index finger and thumb, like this.

Kiki stopped dancing whenever she did it. And she even caused a pileup. Here's what that looked like:

The pileup made us all laugh so hard — even Kiki!

Okay, Diary . . . now that everyone has gone home, I HAVE to draw my comic strip! It's <u>DUE TOMORROW</u>! WAIT A SECOND.

I finally figured out what to do for my comic strip! I don't know why it took me so long to think of this . . . it was <u>SO</u> obvious!

Okay, Diary . . . I've finally finished drawing my comic strip! All that dancing and drawing and thinking takes a lot out of a girl!

NIGHTY NIGHT

Chapter 12

Sweet Dreams

Monday

Sorry I didn't get to write this morning,
Diary. But I just got home from school, so
here's a quick update . . .

We turned in our final newspaper projects
at the end of the day today. Again, Katy
peeked at my
comic strip as
I stood in line
to hand it to
Miss Humphries.

"That's such a cool comic strip." — Katy

I tried to think of something friendly to say back, but she walked away before I could say anything. It's weird that the only person who'll have seen my comic strip before it gets printed in the newspaper is Katy — a person who may or may not be my friend. I hope everyone else will like it when the newspaper is passed out on Wednesday.

Okay — off to hip-hop class with all my friends. Who ever thought I would have enough friends to say "all my friends" about?

Hip-hop class was SO great. And the LLGs were really thankful that Jada and I had helped them learn the routine yesterday. They seemed like old **pros** to the rest of the class!

PROS = short for "professionals"

When I got home from class, there was a surprise on the table: foods from all over the world for dinner and dessert! There was way too much for us Maedas to eat on our own (even with Grandma Maeda, who <u>loves</u> her dessert!). So I invited the girls over to help us eat everything.

apple pie

cupcakes

croissants

Pasta

We had so much fun together. And
I'm so lucky my dad is a **chef**!

CHEF =
a cook

Diary, does it bother you when I talk about
food? Because . . . well . . . you can't have any?
I'll stop now.

Sweet dreams.

Chapter 13

So Much Happiness

Tuesday

Good morning, Diary!

I owe you a <u>BIG</u> thank you for sticking
with me through all my worrying.
I promise to repay you with
happier thoughts from now on.

Must go to school.
Have a happy day!

I had so much fun with the LLGs and Jada at school today. I just really hope everyone likes my comic when they see it in the newspaper tomorrow. . . . But don't worry, Diary . . . I'm not nervous. I'm just a happy person, writing happy thoughts! 😊

I have to run to Doggie Day Spa. Bob is so excited!

Bob has never smelled better in his life! And I must say, for a boy, he looks very handsome in his blue doggie nail polish!

I know I promised I wouldn't worry today. But I am a bit nervous about everyone seeing my comic tomorrow and I do feel sort of bad about having so much fun with the LLGs, knowing that Katy might still be upset.

It must mean something that I still care about Katy's feelings after everything that's happened. Right? I guess the question is whether what it means, is that I should still be her friend . . . ????

Is Katy my friend?

or not?

Have a good night, Diary.

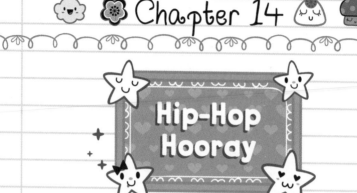

Chapter 14

Wednesday

Diary, I'm so excited! The
school newspaper comes
out TODAY! I can't wait to
see it – and to see what everyone thinks of
my comic! EEEEEKKKK!

At least Katy had said she liked it. Unless she
was just saying that because she wants us
to be friends again.

Send good thoughts today!

The newspaper turned out so great! My friends' newspaper projects were awesome. Even Katy's events calendar looked good!

And . . . everybody loved my comic! Seeing my comic in print and hearing how much everyone liked it, made me realize that Katy really was trying to be a good friend the other day. She'd seen that I was feeling nervous about handing in my project, and what she'd said to me about it was **genuine.**

GENUINE = to be real, truthful, honest

I want to try being friends with Katy again.
So I walked home with her after school today. . . .

"I . . . uh . . . kind of miss being friends with you, Katy." — me

"I miss you, too, mika." — Katy

"If we become friends again, can you maybe try being friendlier to Kiki, Coco, and Lulu?" — me

"Would I have to be friends with them, though?" — Katy

(This worried me a little.)

"No. Nobody <u>has</u> to be anyone's friend. . . . maybe you'll want to be friends with my friends, and maybe you won't. But we really should all be nice to one another."
— me

"I guess I can do that." — Katy

"And, well, I thought it might be fun if you came to our hip-hop class on Monday. You could maybe get to know everyone a little better while doing something really fun with me, too." — me

Katy's face lit up right away.

"I'd love to come to hip-hop with you guys, Mika!" — Katy

It looks like hip-hop class is about to get another new dancer! And I have my comic strip to thank for it. When I saw my comic in the newspaper, it looked like something was missing. So I drew Katy into it. That's when I knew it was finished! Kiki, Coco, Lulu, and Jada liked it, too. Check it out:

GET TO KNOW THE
LOTUS LANE GIRLS!

Kyla May

lives near the beach in Australia with her husband,
three daughters, two dogs, two cats, and four
guinea pigs.

Like Mika, Kyla loves dance! Ballet was one of Kyla's
favorite activities as a kid. And now, her three
daughters love dancing just as much as she did!
As well as dancing, Kyla adores Japan. Whenever
Kyla visits Japan, she is inspired by the amazing
fashion and creativity she sees there. After a
visit to Japan, Kyla is sure to come home with
loads of kawaii toys for her daughters!

Kyla's first passion is drawing. Her second is
chocolate.